WITHDRAWN

KT-461-291

B000 000 021 4336

ABERDEEN LIBRARIES

Fussy Freda

by Julia Jarman and Fred Blunt

There was a girl called Fussy Freda
whose mum and dad tried hard to feed her.

CROAKO
pops

But it didn't matter what they cooked,
Freda only shouted, 'YUK! YUK! YUK!

I don't like
cabbage,

I don't like
beans,

I don't like
anything

coloured **green.**'

Her mother tried

and tried to
feed her,

but **nothing** she
cooked suited Freda.

She tried new recipes but came unstuck

when Freda
only shouted,

'YUK!

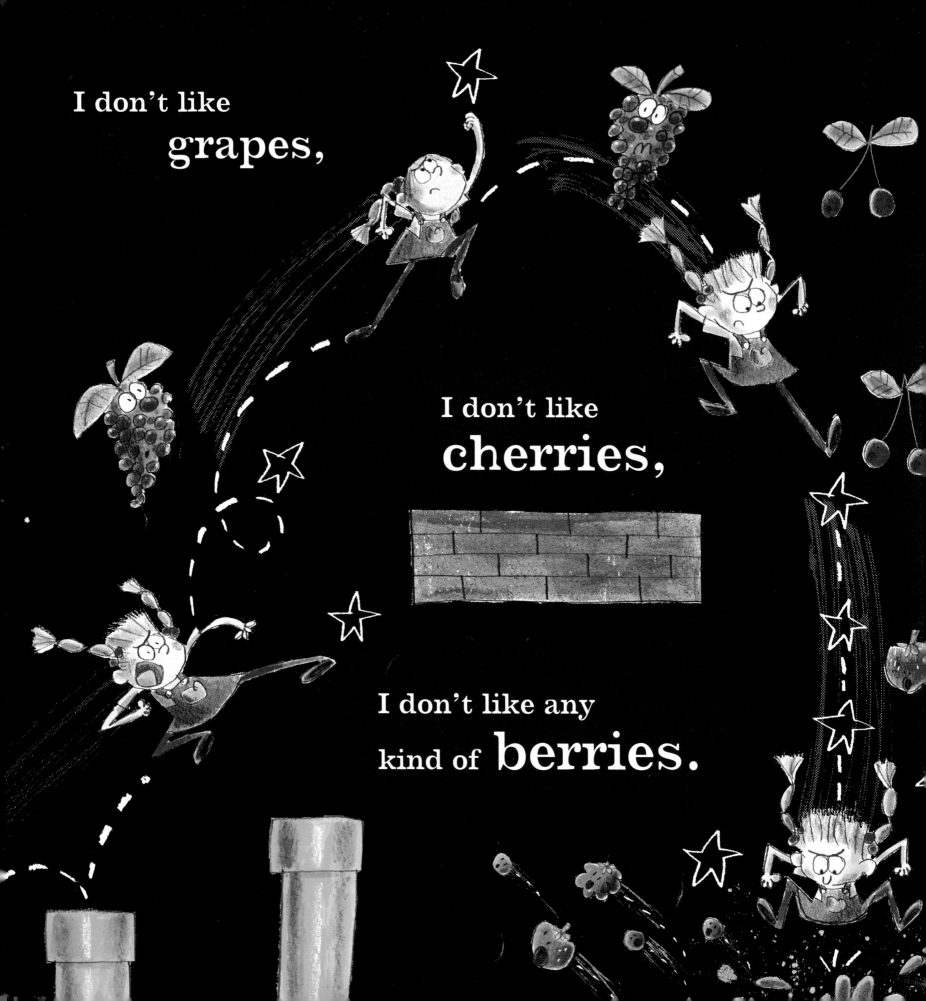

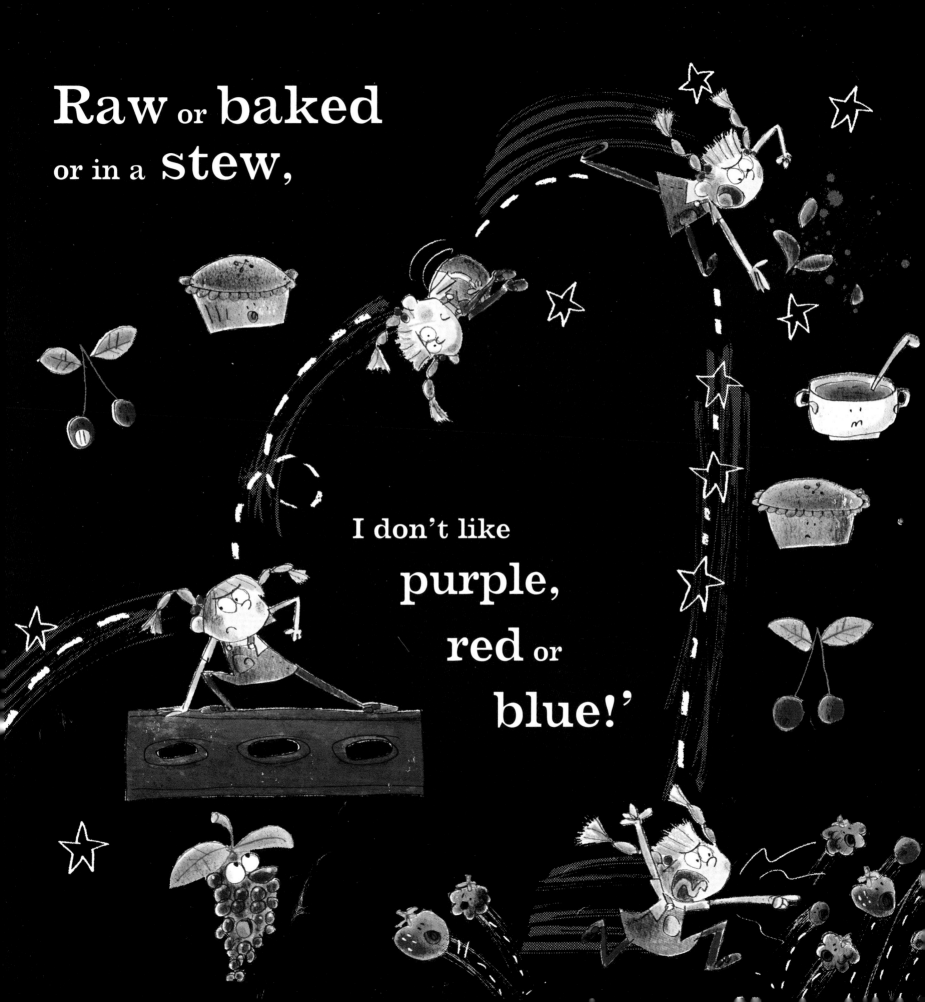

Raw or baked or in a stew,

I don't like purple, red or blue!'

Her father tried his best to feed her,
but nothing suited **Fussy Freda.**

He cooked
her **Chinese
crispy duck,**

Grandma said that she would feed her.
'Fish and chips might tempt our Freda.'

The Cod Father

With fingers crossed Mum said, 'Good luck!'
But Freda only shouted, 'Yuk!'

I don't like **cod.**

I don't like **hake.**

I won't eat **fish,** it makes me *shake.*'

Her aunt and uncle came to stay
with food from their French holiday.

But Freda wouldn't eat or drink.
She refused it all and began to. . .

. . .shrink!

Freda got
shorter

and
shorter

and
shorter!

One day Father said, 'Where is our daughter?'

They found her playing in her doll's house,

where
Claws the
Cat thought
he saw a
mouse!

Mother cried out, 'That's Freda, Claws!'
But the cat had closed his hungry jaws.

**WAS THAT THE END OF
FUSSY FREDA WHOSE PARENTS
TRIED AND TRIED TO FEED HER?**

Well, from the cat
There came a shout.

'YUK!'

he yowled,

and spat Freda out!

'Give me something to eat,' she said.

'W-what would you like?'
they asked with dread.

'Oh, anything,'
sighed Freda. 'Oh!
I want to eat and I
want to grow!'

She ate **saucy beans**

and **buttered toast.**

She ate **spaghetti,**

she ate a **roast.**

She ate **red cherries**

and **rich brown stew,**

and Freda
grew

and
grew

and

GREW!

And what is more she started to cook –

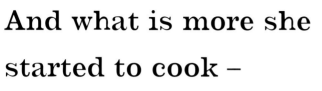

stir-fries,

sausages

and **crispy duck.**

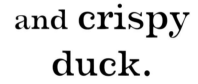

Pancakes,

pizzas,

pasta bake.

Casseroles

and **chocolate cake.**

She's writing her very own **recipe book,**

and she never – well hardly ever – says

'YUK!'

HODDER CHILDREN'S BOOKS

First published in Great Britain in 2017 by Hodder and Stoughton

Text copyright © Julia Jarman, 2017
Illustrations copyright © Fred Blunt, 2017

The moral rights of the author and illustrator have been asserted.

All rights reserved

A CIP catalogue record for this book
is available from the British Library.

ISBN: 978 1 444 92922 5

10 9 8 7 6 5 4 3 2 1

Printed and bound in China

MIX
Paper from
responsible sources
FSC® C104740

Hodder Children's Books
An imprint of Hachette Children's Group
Part of Hodder and Stoughton
Carmelite House, 50 Victoria Embankment
London, EC4Y 0DZ

An Hachette UK Company
www.hachette.co.uk

www.hachettechildrens.co.uk